BEYOND ESCAPE!

BY R.A. MONTGOMERY

ILLUSTRATED BY FRANK BOLLE

BANTAM BOOKS
TORONTO · NEW YORK · LONDON · SYDNEY · AUCKLAND

RL 5, IL age 10 and up

BEYOND ESCAPE!
A Bantam Book / October 1986

*CHOOSE YOUR OWN ADVENTURE™ is a registered trademark of
Bantam Books, Inc. Registered in U.S. Patent and Trademark
Office and elsewhere.*

Original conception of Edward Packard

ISBN 0-553-26169-X

Published simultaneously in the United States and Canada

Bantam Books are published by Bantam Books. Inc. Its trademark, consisting of the words "Bantam Books" and the por-
trayal of a rooster, is Registered in U.S. Patent and Trademark
Office and in other countries. Marca Registrada. Bantam
Books, Inc., 666 Fifth Avenue, New York, New York 10103.

PRINTED IN THE UNITED STATES OF AMERICA

O   0 9 8 7 6 5 4 3 2 1

BEYOND ESCAPE!

WARNING!!!

Do not read this book straight through from beginning to end! These pages contain many different adventures you can have in the year 2041 as you protect the security of your country. From time to time as you read along, you will be asked to make decisions and choices. Your choices may lead to success or disaster! The adventures you have will be the result of the choices you make. After you make a choice, follow the directions to see what happens to you next.

Think carefully before you make a move. A hostile region borders your country, and your mission may be dangerous at times!

Good luck!

You are Chief of Operations for all activities outside the borders of Turtalia. Turtalia is a democratic country that was formed in the early part of the twenty-first century after domestic and foreign wars split up what was then called the United States.

Turtalia is made up of the former mountain states north of Arizona and the northern plains states, extending into Canada. Its capital is Denver. Turtalia is bordered to the south and east by the hostile totalitarian state called Dorado, to the west by an untamed land, and to the east by a haphazard jumble of quarrelsome states called Rebellium. After winning a vicious war, Turtalia had tried to pacify Dorado. But the Doradans broke away soon after their defeat, and they continue to be a source of danger to Turtalia.

Turn to page 2.

You're one of the true Turtalian heroes. During the difficult Doradan Wars, you led a secret mission to Dorado to obtain their invasion plans. You succeeded, and Turtalia foiled the Doradans in their attempted takeover. You wear with pride the gold and silver ribbon, symbol of Turtalia's highest respect and love. Only two others have the right to the ribbon. Neither is alive.

The year is 2041. The Doradans have been strangely quiet for the last two years—a sure sign of trouble, you think.

It's your responsibility to find out what's going on outside Turtalian borders and to prevent any new attacks on your country. Not long ago, you sent two of your best agents, Mimla and Matt, to check on the situation in the untamed land west of Turtalia. The land, once called California, has been the scene of vicious guerrilla-style fighting, and it's hard to follow what's going on there.

Initial reports from Matt and Mimla indicate that the Doradans might be working with some of the Californians, planning to use the area to stage a new attack on Turtalia. But your agents have failed to make their last three radio contacts with Operations Center in Denver. When last heard from, they were some one hundred miles due east of what used to be the city of San Francisco.

Turn to page 5.

No one answers.

"Nothing! Absolutely nothing," you say, angry at your failure to contact anyone and worried that you might well have given away your position.

You turn your attention back to flying and realize that you haven't been careful about watching your altimeter and airspeed while you tried the radio. Now, suddenly, you discover that you're below four thousand feet, and your airspeed has dropped almost to stall speed!

The control surfaces begin to flutter and the stick becomes sluggish. You increase power and push the nose forward to pick up speed. The plane responds well, but you're now zooming between rolling hills in a narrow valley. Ahead of you looms a much larger, higher hill.

Turn to page 36.

4

"I'm from Turtalia," you explain. "I'm on a mission to rescue two of our people who were last reported in this vicinity."

There's a murmur among the group.

"Quiet! I can't listen and put up with your babbling, too," the leader says to his band. He turns back to you. "How do we know this is true? Can you prove it? None of you people is trustworthy, anyway."

You think for a moment, and then reply, "I can't prove anything. But let me ask, who are you?"

"You've got a lot of spunk. I'll say that for you. Come with us. We'll figure all of this out. My name is Sellers. I'm the leader here."

One of the band stays behind to guard the plane and to search it. Fortunately it's unmarked and carries no military identification.

Turn to page 67.

You're sitting pondering the problem in Operations Center when there's an urgent knock at your door. A lieutenant rushes in. She's red-faced and looks worried.

"Haven has escaped, Commander!"

"What?" you shout, jumping to your feet. Haven is a Doradan spy! "When? How?"

"Sometime early this morning. And that's not all! Three top-secret files are missing from Central Computer Office!"

Before you can fully digest what the lieutenant has said, another officer enters the room. He hands you a piece of computer paper. Your eyes scan the printout:

IN TROUBLE—EXTREMELY IMPORTANT INFORMATION FOR YOU—NO TIME— HURRY IF YOU CAN—WE ARE—

"I think it's from Matt and Mimla," the second officer says.

What next? you wonder.

If you decide to go after Haven and the missing top-secret files, turn to page 9.

If you decide to find Matt and Mimla, turn to page 87.

Your helicopter is one of the new generation of high-speed, low-noise craft. The pilot is experienced and talented. Soon, you're at an altitude of two thousand feet, busily scanning the horizon with computer-enhanced binoculars capable of enlarging an image seventy times. They also pick up radiation from living creatures.

You're in constant contact with the forces on the ground led by Captain Ricardo and the ranger lieutenant who had spoken earlier at the meeting.

Suddenly, clouds envelop your helicopter, and radio communication is knocked out. The clouds contain a choking, blinding gas. You and your pilot reach for the oxygen equipment, but the pilot slumps forward and stops breathing. A crimson circle appears on his uniform over his heart. He's dead!

If you try to land the helicopter yourself, turn to page 16.

If you decide to bail out, turn to page 80.

"You might as well give up on your friends for dead," says another Rebel. "Sellers pushes the limits all the time."

"Can I get to this other camp?" you ask.

"Sure," the Rebel answers. "In fact, we'll take you part of the way. You can join the patrol that's heading out shortly."

You're escorted by a party of four armed people, three women and one man, to a spot where you can see a range of rolling hills beyond an immense stretch of land.

"Sellers is out there," they say, pointing to the hills. "You're on your own now. Good luck."

Two days later, you're stopped by a Rebel guard. He leads you to Sellers inside the camp, which is under heavy attack by Doradans and Corporation troops.

You explain who you are.

"So where are they?" you ask Sellers.

"Where are who?"

"Matt and Mimla," you say impatiently.

Sellers shrugs.

"I was told they were here."

"You were told wrong. And I suggest you get out of here. The fighting's heavy. You'd be better off on your own."

You think about that for a moment. At last you make a decision.

Turn to page 35.

In questioning the lieutenant who reported Haven's escape, you learn that he drugged his guards with herbs he found growing in the prison-farm fields. The prison farm is adjacent to Operations Center. How Haven got the top-secret files is anyone's guess, but it seems likely that there are Doradan agents in the Turtalian forces who gave him a hand. That's an unpleasant, but real, part of the tangled political situation that now exists— spies are everywhere.

Haven's escape occurred several hours ago.

"I'll have to act quickly," you say to yourself. You try your best to push Mimla and Matt from your mind. They could be in serious danger, but you know you have to handle one thing at a time.

You press the full-emergency-warning button that sits on your desk. You have command of a helicopter fleet and a ranger force of highly trained trackers and climbers. All the people in your command are dedicated, or so you hope.

Turn to page 14.

"Let's see what the day brings, Sellers. It's never good to make a decision when you have an empty stomach and a tired body." You yawn and stretch.

Sellers nods and gives commands to some of his people. Moments later you're given the herb tea he mentioned, a good cup of chamomile tea, and a stew, probably rabbit. It's hot, nourishing, and delicious. Then you're handed a down sleeping bag patched many times in a crazy quilt pattern of fabrics. Finally, you lie down inside the tent assigned to you, and stare out through the tent flap. The sky is clear now and dawn is not far off. The soft grass beneath you is a welcome mattress. Outside your tent a woman sits cross-legged with a weapon on her lap. She's your guard, but also your protector.

Turn to page 25.

"If we really are surrounded, then we don't stand a chance in daylight," you say. "The plane is slow on climbout, particularly with three of us aboard. Let's see what we can do about hiding it."

Matt and Mimla agree, but Sellers mutters, "Your funeral. I think you should go while the going's good, but do as you wish." He gives several commands, and several of his people go off and hide the plane. You, Matt, and Mimla sit and talk. They tell you that the Doradans have formed an alliance with the Corporation and that an air attack on Turtalia from the west is inevitable. Parachute troops will be used. The attack is to be coordinated with an attack on Turtalia from Dorado in the south. "Even now, Doradan troop planes are arriving here, to be ready for the attack. I'm afraid nothing will stop them," Matt says.

"Let's use the radio," Mimla suggests. "We can contact Operations Center right away." But you don't want to risk alerting the Doradans that their plans for a coordinated surprise attack are known. "Our communications are too easy to intercept," you say. "We'd better concentrate on getting back to Operations Center as fast as possible after dark. We can launch a commando-style raid from there."

Turn to page 88.

A squad of Doradan troops moves forward cautiously. You, Sellers, and the others who are still alive lay down your weapons.

"You will come with us," the Doradan officer in charge says. "We'll find out what you know and who you are."

You wonder if Matt and Mimla met a similar fate. Maybe they're still alive, and are prisoners of this same group of Doradans. You may even join them soon. Then it will be up to you to plan an escape.

The End

"Okay, people, here's the plan," you announce to the five officers who came rushing to your office in response to the warning bell. "Haven can't have gotten too far. We're surrounded by miles of semi-desert prairie. No vehicles are missing from the motor pool, and no strange aircraft have been reported in the area." You pause for a moment.

"Commander, how can we be so sure that he's out there?" a lieutenant wearing the sand-colored camouflage uniform of the rangers asks. "Maybe he never left the compound. Has it been searched?"

Another officer jumps in before you can answer.

"The compound's been searched from turnip to washcloth. He's not there."

"Well, we'll leave a detail here to assure that, if Haven is hiding, he'll be caught the minute he surfaces. Thank you both." You nod at them and continue.

"I'll take the lead helicopter and direct the search of the territory due south from the air. Captain Ricardo, you take the rangers and spread out in a southerly direction."

Turn to page 7.

"Yes," you answer. "I know the President and the Peace Coordinator have ordered me to give up solo missions, but this is different. It's the kind of mission I can do better on my own. And the information our agents have uncovered may be vital to us. The President can reprimand me when I get back."

"If you get back," the lieutenant replies.

"Enough of that kind of talk. I'd better get going." You feel a slight tug of fear as you leave the security of your office in Operations Center and head for the airfield. It's been a long time since you've gone on a solo mission.

At the airfield, you pick up the survival kit bag you keep prepared for just such occasions. As you stow the kit bag in the sleek, new three-person motorglider, you feel a thrill of excitement. It's good to be back in action, you think.

Fifteen minutes later, you clear ground control and climb out into the blue Turtalian skies. The plane responds well to the controls, and you gain altitude rapidly. Soon you're heading for the northern part of what used to be California. Your airspeed is one hundred and twenty knots. The wind is from the northwest at ten to fifteen miles per hour. You calculate an ETA at eight hours from now.

Turn to page 18.

The helicopter dips and swerves in a half-loop until you stabilize it. You use a combination of rotor speed and emergency jet thrusters to bring it under control. Frantically, you key the mike, hoping radio communication has been restored.

"Come in, Ranger Three. Mayday! Mayday!"

There's no response, not even the usual static crackle. Looking at the control panel, you see that the radio's been destroyed. It must have been hit in the same attack that killed the pilot. But how did it happen? You haven't heard or seen any enemy aircraft.

Just then, when you thought you had the helicopter under control, it pitches and yaws again in a violent swing.

Suddenly you see them! In a tight formation in front of your helicopter are three disklike shapes moving at a slow speed. They have a luminescent quality, as if the sun were shining through them or reflecting onto them from water.

Zam!

A bright light flashes to the port side of the helicopter.

Turn to page 102.

Once you've made up your mind, you set yourself for action. Your body tenses, preparing to release its energy in one smooth, swift blow.

Slowly you reach down, pretending your bootlace has come undone. Haven seems unconcerned. You kneel on the sandy ground, fumble with your lace, and prepare for the move to grasp the metal rod. You can hear your heartbeat.

Turn to page 84.

Even though you're chasing the retreating sun, you lose—night envelops you and the land. Only on the distant horizon is there an aura of yellow and crimson. Then that, too, is gone, and clouds play games with the stars. Below you stretch miles of darkened land. Occasionally, flickering lights appear, probably fires at campsites. But you're not sure whether the fires are from Rebel bases, Doradan army outposts, or the camps of hunters or sheepherders.

Finally, you're over the area where Matt and Mimla's last message was broadcast from. To the west you see the blinking lights of yet another campsite. Beyond is San Francisco. In what remains of San Francisco, there's an underground network that was established several years before. Maybe someone from the underground could help in your search for Matt and Mimla.

If you think an investigation of the campfires below will lead you to your agents, turn to page 26.

If you decide to try to contact the underground, turn to page 23.

"I caution you to use great care in your strike against the Doradans," Haven continues. "Devastation is an outmoded and useless policy. We can help you to avoid extreme measures by using the technology we have aboard this craft." Haven looks at Marileva and then at you. "We are able to neutralize without causing damage," he says quietly.

"It would be the answer to our prayers to end this conflict without killing," you say. "But how do you 'neutralize' your enemies?"

Turn to page 34.

"Climb aboard!" you say to Sellers early the next morning, when the two of you have returned to your motorglider. "Let's just hope you know where we're going."

"I do. Anyway, I've always believed that everyone has the right to fail. If we don't try, there's no chance to succeed. Trust me." He buckles himself into the plane, and you close the canopy. Moments later you're airborne.

Sellers looks down and smiles. "We were surrounded, you know," he says.

"What? You mean down there?" you reply in horror at the idea that you've just made a takeoff in a valley surrounded by hostile troops who could have easily blown you out of the sky.

"Well, they didn't know they had us surrounded, but they did. Four or five Doradan and Corporation patrols are out there. We've been watching them, waiting for our chance to get out. With luck, we can stay one jump ahead of them." Sellers stops talking and again looks out at the seemingly peaceful world below.

Turn to page 40.

You bend your knees as you hit the ground, and the shock is far less than you'd expected.

"These new para-foil chutes are great," you announce, even though no one's around to hear your praise of the new parachute technology.

You key your miniature communicator, standard equipment for all Turtalian forces. You hope it works.

"Red Leader to Ranger Three. Come in," you say, hoping desperately for a reply. "Red Leader. Repeat, Red Leader. Where are you, Ranger Three?" You look around for some sign of people on the deserted prairie. But all communication is dead, just as it was in the helicopter. And not a soul is in sight.

A whining sound interrupts your concentration. Looking up, you see an enormous silvery shape rapidly coming your way. It blocks the sun. You're in the shadow of a device unknown to you.

Turn to page 30.

At your present airspeed you'll reach San Francisco in an hour. Turtalian intelligence gave you the name of a man there who may be able to help you trace the actions and movements of Matt and Mimla. He might even guide you to the area where Matt and Mimla transmitted that last message.

There's a slight headwind, but the flying is easy. The campfires below fade from view. Soon you're soaring over the mountains and starting to descend toward San Francisco.

Reports in Turtalia have indicated that San Francisco and its surrounding areas are divided into three hostile segments. A gang of criminals called the Corporation maintains control of the central part of the city from the docks to the top of Telegraph Hill and out to the Golden Gate Bridge. Or what once was the Golden Gate Bridge—now it's simply jumbled concrete, metal, and cable on either side of the bay, with no bridge spanning the shores.

The Corporation is a mixture of military people, gamblers, and drug dealers, and is headed by the president of a famous high-tech company. He has turned his creative genius to the organization of political power over a once populous and successful city. There is apparent madness in his appetite for raw power.

Turn to page 38.

Sleep comes quickly, perhaps due to drugs in the tea, perhaps due to the fatigue of a long day. Dreams cascade through your head. At one point you're running wildly up, up, up, a steep, sloping path, desperate to gain the top—except that the path goes on forever.

Later you dream that you're back in school, taking exams, but you can't remember what subjects you've studied or what exams you must take. You toss and turn, thrashing inside the narrow sleeping bag. Then you dream that you've found Matt and Mimla. This dream seems very real. Only you can't understand why Mimla is shaking you.

Turn to page 83.

You put the motorglider into a long, slow banking turn. At eight thousand feet it's very difficult to make out the details of the terrain. You kick the rudder pedal and push the stick over and forward. Your plane sideslips quietly and effortlessly until the altimeter reads six thousand feet. There are rolling hills below, and you feel that this is the safest altitude for now. You level off and cut back on the throttle.

Scanning the country around the campsites, you see ample landing room in grassy open spaces. One field is fairly close to one of the campfires.

"I wonder if I should try radio contact," you say to yourself. "It's risky. It'd be a dead giveaway if those are hostile troops. On the other hand, it would save time and be safer if I could get someone to help check the field before I land."

*If you try to make radio contact,
turn to page 3.*

*If you decide to go in without radio contact,
turn to page 32.*

"Okay, Haven, or whoever you are, I'll take a chance and go aboard this thing of yours." Your curiosity is so great that you can't give up this opportunity to board a spacecraft.

"Fine. I thought you'd agree. You are a thoughtful and intelligent creature, Commander," Haven says.

He reaches out again and takes your hand. Seconds later you materialize inside the craft. Nothing about the outside of the silvery craft, with its smooth, metallic skin, prepared you for what you'd find inside. You look around in surprise at the glasslike, many-faceted space. It's like being inside a diamond.

"Where are we?" you blurt out, stunned by the brilliant, multicolored light that reflects inwardly from the facets.

"We are within a complex carbon atom that has been enlarged to a size appropriate for earth voyaging," replies a creature that has appeared beside Haven. The creature is square, sharp-edged, metallic gray, with red plastic fittings.

Before your eyes it develops mechanical arms and legs, a body and a head. It reminds you of something you've read about—the Japanese "transformer" toys that were so popular years ago in the former United States.

Turn to page 47.

"Look, I'm just an ordinary civilian. My brother's been living outside of San Francisco for years. He moved there before the bad times. I'm trying to find him. I want . . ."

"Stop right there," the man with the lamp says. "You look honest. I follow instincts. I don't believe your story, but for some oddball reason, I trust you. I'm called Sellers, and these are—"

Just then an owl hoots. Sellers holds his hand up.

"Quiet!" he whispers to you. "That's one of my people. There could be company we don't need or want around here."

Two shots are fired. They're accurate: two of the civilians near you slump to the ground.

"Hold your fire," Sellers yells to his people. "Every shot must count." He grabs you by the arm and pulls you down behind a jumble of boulders.

"Here, use this if you want," he says, handing you an automatic weapon. He also hands you two clips of ammunition. "We Rebels don't have much ammunition, so use it carefully."

Go on to the next page.

Bullets fill the air. You look toward your plane just in time to see a barrage of bullets slam into it. There's a muffled *whump* as the gas tank explodes. In minutes your plane becomes a twisted, ugly, black tangle of metal and melted plastic.

Sellers grabs your arm again.

"Sorry about all this. You may be better off on your own."

If you decide to slip away on your own,
turn to page 33.

If you decide to stay with Sellers,
turn to page 35.

There's no place to hide.

A beam of sky-blue light reaches down from the underside of the object and bathes you in its warm energy. You try to move, to step out of the beam. But your feet are locked in position! You try to raise your arm, but it remains at your side. Your breathing slows, and your pulse rate falls until your heart is beating so slowly that you can feel each pulse in its full rhythmic movement.

In rapid stages Haven materializes beside you—first his head and shoulders, then his whole body. Slowly, facial details and coloration are added. The apparition reaches out and touches you—and the touch releases you from the frozen state you've been in. Haven speaks.

Turn to page 41.

You scan your instruments, automatically checking your airspeed and altimeter reading. Landing on an unknown field can be tricky. "But not as tricky as using the radio when there may be Doradans around," you remind yourself. The crackle of your voice in the dimly lit cabin of the motorglider sounds unreal to you.

You repeatedly scan the sky for other aircraft and watch the clouds as they pass between you and the land. Twice you circle what seems to be the best landing spot. Then you set up for landing and begin the final approach.

Flaps down, airspeed correct, wings level, you think, staring into the fast-approaching dark area of grassy field. Your plane pitches and rolls in changing air. You move the controls gingerly but knowingly.

Turn to page 46.

"You may be right, Sellers. Good-bye and good luck. I hope you make it," you tell him.

"Yeah, see you around," he replies and then turns to the job at hand.

You saw where your kit bag was dropped when the shooting started, and you're able to find it in the dark. All around you people are fighting for their lives. You wonder how many others will try to slip away into the night and escape the madness of gunfire.

You shrug into the shoulder straps of the kit bag and crawl back from the ring of fire, moving like a snail, hoping to get away unnoticed.

The intensity of gunfire eases, and you rise to a crouching position. Then you begin to run, bent low over the ground. Nothing happens! You're still alive. You haven't been seen.

You cover a hundred yards, stop, catch your breath, then travel another hundreds yards, and stop again. Gunfire erupts with renewed fierceness. You now hear the persistent and ominous thump of mortar rounds. Cries of pain and terror are carried through the night air. You keep going.

Turn to page 86.

Before Haven can reply, Marileva interrupts.

"The Turtalian Congress has replied in the affirmative," she announces, switching off her communicator. "The preemptive strike should be launched as soon as possible."

"Leave it to me," Haven replies and gives commands to his crew to guide the spacecraft to the Doradan capital. "We will stop the threat without harming anyone. Then it is up to you to change what is going on in Dorado. We could be a good team, you Earthlings and we Crystal People. As I said before, we need your help, too. We will talk about that later. By the way, here are your top-secret files. We have no need of them. I took them only so that I could lure you to me."

The End

"I'm staying, Sellers," you say. "I'm determined to do what I came to do. Anyway, you need all the help you can get."

"Fine, but, remember, it's your neck," he replies.

The fighting is intense, and you're too busy defending your life to search for Matt and Mimla. There seems little hope of getting out alive. You think about your life in Turtalia and what the freedom of choice has meant for your people. The firing eases at times, and hope renews at these moments.

"I can't see who we're fighting," you say to Sellers.

"It's always like that," he replies. "Ambushes, hit and run. Actually, we use the same tactics. All the same, it just means killing people."

Shortly after, the firing begins again. It seems impossible that anyone will survive the awful violence.

Suddenly you're out of ammunition!

Turn to page 39.

"Yikes!" you yell as you pull back on the stick, giving the plane full throttle. You barely make it over the crest of the hill.

"That would've been a dumb way to die. I've got to get a grip on myself, or else I'll never find Matt and Mimla."

At that moment a heat-seeking rocket rises from one of the campsites below.

The small fireball from your exploding plane is greeted with great joy by the Doradan patrol that launched the rockets.

The End

Intelligence reports also have indicated that factions within the Corporation want the President out, indeed, want him dead. But he seems to have a genius for survival. He's unpredictable, unfair, and brilliant.

The other two groups in and around San Francisco are resistance groups fighting the Corporation. They vie with one another for the support of a dazed, poverty-stricken, and frightened population. One group is called the Rebels; the other changes its name about as often as the weather changes. Your contact is a member of the Rebels.

The airport for which you're heading is in a disputed area. Since your plane can also land in a small field, you decide against trying the airport and instead look for the playing fields on the Berkeley campus. The university is closed, of course, and it lies in the district on San Francisco Bay reported to be under the control of the Rebels.

Turn to page 43.

"Sellers, I'm out. Have you got any more clips?"

"Nope. That's it, I'm afraid. I ran out minutes ago myself."

Soon all of the Rebels are out of ammunition. The attackers sense what has happened, but they're cautious. They hold their positions, suspecting the Rebels might be bluffing.

Finally, they contact you through a loudspeaker.

"Throw down your arms! There is no alternative. I repeat, stand up and throw down your weapons!"

Sellers nods and shrugs his shoulders. "Let's see what happens."

Turn to page 12.

Blindly you follow the directions Sellers gives you. "I hope we're getting close," you tell him after you've been flying for some time. "Looks like bad weather ahead." He nods silently, and you turn your attention back to your flying.

Soon the sky is filled with towering thunderheads capable of ripping the wings off any airplane and especially off the delicate motorglider you're flying. You dodge in and out of the clouds, climbing, diving, banking, and turning. Lightning flashes all around you, illuminating the clouds as though someone were switching on lamps inside them. The wind currents at twelve thousand feet are gusting well over forty knots, and your plane is tossed around the sky.

You fly on and on, battling to stay in the air. Twice you slip through the clouds looking for a place to land, but without success.

Turn to page 56.

"I am certain you did not expect this, did you? I have more power than you imagined." Haven's tone is slow and even. There's no harshness in his voice.

You nod your head. He continues.

"I have never been a Doradan, you know. Actually, I am not human. You can tell by my craft here. I am of a society called the Crystal People. And the people of my world need the help of the people of your world. I could not be sure whether the Doradans or you Turtalians should be the ones to help. I have now decided—on the people of Turtalia. Will you come aboard my craft and find out what we need? We are friendly."

"What happens if I refuse?" you reply.

"Nothing at all. You are free to go."

"What about my pilot? If you're so friendly, why did you kill him?" you ask.

"It was not us who killed your pilot. Are you sure your own people are reliable?" Haven replies.

At that moment you catch sight of three figures moving toward you in the distance. They're members of the Turtalian ranger force.

If you decide to trust Haven for the time being, turn to page 27.

If you decide to make a dash for freedom and join your own people, turn to page 44.

Minutes later you spot the football field and decide from a careful check that it's probably safe to land there. You don't try making radio contact.

The landing is easy. The plane comes to a stop at the midpoint of the field. No one is about. You climb out of the cockpit, grab your kit bag, and head out to find the man named Jeremy, your Rebel contact.

Turn to page 89.

You drop to the ground, knocking Haven down with a kick to his legs. Before he can respond, you're on your feet and running in the direction of the three rangers.

"Don't fire. It's me!" you shout. But they're too far away to identify you. They watch your approach warily.

You run as hard as you can. There's no looking back. At any moment you expect a shot or a paralyzing ray to hit you. Haven won't give me up too easily, you think.

But no shot rings out. No paralyzing ray stops you. Ahead the rangers stand with weapons at the ready. You make one final burst forward and reach the safety of the group of rangers.

"Thank heavens you're here," you gasp. "I've never been so happy—" You stop when you see their grim faces. You suddenly realize that no one has moved forward to help you.

"Don't move, Commander. You can't escape," says a lieutenant newly assigned to the ranger force.

"Don't move or you'll never move again."

"What do you mean?" you cry. "Drop those weapons! Don't you dare aim them at me!"

Turn to page 50.

"Okay! Okay! I'm not moving," you say. Fear makes your voice sound feeble and thin.

"Now, step down slowly. Drop the bag on the ground. Hands up," the voice says in a slow, assured tone.

You do as it says. You have no choice.

"Stop right there," the voice commands.

Moments later you're surrounded by five people dressed in civilian clothes. One of them picks up your kit bag. The man who gave the commands illuminates a small lamp and looks at you. He speaks again.

"If you're a Doradan, you can count the moments left in your life on both hands. If you're not, you'd better do some fast talking."

If you tell your captors who you really are and explain about Matt and Mimla, turn to page 4.

If you pretend you're a civilian trying to locate your brother who lived outside of San Francisco, turn to page 28.

The wheels of your motorglider touch the earth. The plane rolls through the grass, bumping across uneven ground. You kick the rudder pedals several times, trying to avoid what looks like rocks or bumps in the terrain. Your efforts don't do much good.

With one last jolt, the plane comes to a stop.

"Not bad," you congratulate yourself as you unlatch the canopy. Cool, fragrant night air rushes over you. You stretch, then unsnap your seat belt and shoulder harness. You flick off the switches, and the plane becomes a silent, motionless piece of the landscape.

Your survival kit is in the backseat. You reach around, pick it up, and step out of the cockpit and onto the wing.

"Don't move or you're dead." The voice from the darkness startles you. You hear the unmistakable click of an automatic weapon going from safety to full automatic.

Turn to page 45.

"You certainly are a changeable sort, aren't you?" you say nervously to your new companion.

Haven chuckles and crosses his arms, leaning back against a crystal wall.

"Just watch." The robotlike creature begins to soften, the metallic gray changes to flesh tones, the mechanical arms and legs become soft, flexible, and finally there's an earth-type person standing next to you. This person, dressed in the conventional unisex clothes common to Turtalia, smiles and says, "Not bad for a beginner, is it?"

Turning to Haven, you ask, "What is it you want of us here on Earth? What do we have that you don't?"

Haven looks at you and replies in a calm, measured tone, "We need two things: first, a secret operations base to house our attack arm. We are at war with the neighboring galaxy."

"What else?" you ask.

"A home for our people if or when we must leave our planet. We need your help to convince the Turtalian Congress to aid us. The Doradans are too paranoid and selfish to help anyone." Haven waits for your reply.

*If you decide to take up Haven's cause,
turn to page 51.*

*If you stall for time and try to leave the crystal,
turn to page 70.*

"Watch it, Marileva," you yell as two Doradan guards drop to their knees, firing their weapons on full automatic. Just then a member of your ranger force hurls a smoke grenade. Two others overpower the guards, and you, Marileva, and three rangers rush into the building.

You know the layout of the Doradan operations building very well. When you were captured during the Doradan Wars several years ago, you were often brought here for interrogation.

"Second floor, third door, Marileva," you yell. "Watch out!"

You kick the door open with one massive swing of your foot.

Turn to page 76.

The lieutenant motions to one of the others, who snaps handcuffs on your wrists. From behind some scrub pine a squad of soldiers emerges, wearing the uniform of the Doradan army!

"Well done, Lieutenant!" Haven says. He has suddenly appeared at your side. "Leave this Earthling to me."

The ranger lieutenant snaps a salute and turns to talk with the Doradans.

"Where are my troops?" you ask, dreading the answer.

"We've taken care of them, don't worry," replies the turncoat lieutenant.

Haven leads you back toward the spacecraft.

"So, you've won after all, haven't you, Haven?" you say in a disgusted tone.

"Be calm, Commander. Nothing is ever what it appears to be. I am as anxious to be free of these Doradans as you are. They are fascists. Our intelligence has analyzed their system; fascism will not work in the long run. As I told you, we need help, and we want it from you Turtalians. Will you contact your home base and report our position? Your forces can capture the Doradans, and we can begin discussions on how to help one another."

If you use your communicator to contact Operations Center, turn to page 54.

If you decide to fake the communication, turn to page 58.

"For some reason I believe you, Haven, despite your past history of having helped the Doradans. After all, you didn't know how bad the Doradans really are. First, though, tell me more. I need to know all about you."

"It will take time, Commander, unless you will allow me to do a Rapid Information Transfer with our crystal circuit."

"I don't know. My circuits are humanoid; they might not interface with yours," you reply.

"Do not worry," Haven says. "We have analyzed the human construction and will tap in appropriately."

Turn to page 63.

"Morning. Nice day," you say, hoping nonchalance will break the ice. You move toward the counter.

"Coffee, please."

"No coffee. What do you think we are, a civilized nation, bud? It's herb tea, like it or lump it. That's all we've got. That's all we've had for seven long years."

"Fine. That will do just fine."

You sit huddled over the strong, aromatic tea. Finally, you summon your courage. "You wouldn't happen to have an old copy of the *New York Times* around, would you?" you ask the waiter. It's your code, and if the waiter is Jeremy he'll recognize it.

He looks at you and asks, "What date?"

Turn to page 64.

Your call to Operations Center results in an immediate response to your request for help with the Doradans. With little or no firing, a Turtalian strike force rounds up the Doradan team. Your ranger force, being held prisoner two miles from the spacecraft, is quickly located. They'd been immobilized by an old-fashioned gas once used by police to quell protests during the political clashes of the 1960s in the United States. Its effectiveness was temporary, and exposure to the gas caused no residual harm—just tearstained faces.

Aboard the Turtalian command craft is the chief political officer of Turtalia, a woman named Marileva.

"I'm anxious to talk with this being—this Haven—who paraded as the Doradan spy. Where is he?" she asks you.

"Why, right here," you reply. You turn to find that no one is standing beside you. "He was here a minute ago!"

"Have no fear." The voice of Haven floats in the air. "I am just resting for a bit. It is quite fatiguing to be in humanoid form for too long."

Go on to the next page.

His body begins to rematerialize beside you.

"I have information important to you Turtalians," he says. "The Doradans plan to launch a surprise attack on your capital in Denver within the next week. I recommend striking *their* capital first. We can use my forces and my craft. Will you accept our aid?" he asks. "Of course, we want something in return."

If you want to accept, turn to page 59.

If you want to reject his offer of help, turn to page 66.

Time passes in agonizing minutes. Hope for a break in the storm is the only thing that keeps you going. Finally, you enter a cloud so dense and so high that you pray you will get out of it alive.

Your prayer is not answered. You and Sellers and your airplane meet the unyielding rock face of a mountain hidden by the clouds.

The End

"Sure, Haven, I'll contact my home base," you say as you fiddle with the communicator, stalling for time. You have a hunch that Haven is trying to invade your security wavelength and head up a Doradan takeover attack.

Haven nods and turns his back to you to speak rapidly to one of his crew.

Meanwhile the Doradan forces are busy arranging the transport of their prisoners—your ranger force—back to the Doradan territory. They move off, paying little attention to you because they trust Haven and his crew.

Haven seems engrossed in his conversation. Scanning the immediate area you see a metal rod about five feet long lying on the ground.

You think there's a chance for escape if you can knock Haven out, get his weapon, and head for cover in the piñon trees. But only if Haven's crew member returns to the spacecraft, leaving you and Haven alone.

You wait and watch. Haven concludes his talk, dismisses the crew members, and turns back to you. The two of you are now alone. The Doradans are out of sight.

If you decide to knock out Haven, turn to page 17.

If you decide not to use force, turn to page 71.

"Well, we'll need all the help we can get. Those Doradans never give up." You look questioningly at Marileva. She nods in agreement.

"Please ask for permission to lead a preemptive strike on the Doradan capital. An emergency session of Congress should give it to us."

Marileva nods again and uses her communicator, scrambling the message to avoid interception by any Doradan listening posts. Haven invites you and Marileva inside his spacecraft. During the two hours while you anxiously await the Turtalian Congress's okay to proceed with a neutralizing strike against the Doradans, you learn of Haven's home galaxy, which is on the rim of the Outer Seat of Time.

"Do you mean, Haven, that between here and there, with all those billions of planets and stars, only Earth seems like a suitable place for your people?"

Haven is in his humanoid form. He grins and replies, "What seems like impossible numbers of stars and planets to you is a mere trifle to us. But, the answer is yes. Earth is a comfortable place for us. And it is one of the truly hopeful and bright spots in the universe; that is, if you do not destroy yourselves in the way our planet is busy doing," he adds, looking grim.

Turn to page 20.

"You'd better be for real, Haven. Denver will blow us both out of the sky in a microsecond if they suspect treachery." You don't feel secure about the decision, but it seems the best way to get out of the mess you're in.

Haven nods, and you enter his spacecraft. As the craft heads for Denver, you give Haven the proper security codes. Seconds before you arrive, he gives a command to his crew. The beam of azure light that earlier froze your action incapacitates you once again.

Denver base reads Haven's maneuvers as hostile. The Tactical Strike Command fires a circular barrage. You, Haven, and the spacecraft merge with the universe.

The End

"I believe Turtalians share your interests," you answer. "The Corporation is as dangerous to us as the Doradans are. Now that the two are in league, we're all worse off. Yes, we'll give you direct help—people, equipment, supplies. First, though, what about Matt and Mimla? Where are they?"

Jeremy looks at you. He's not a friendly type, you think.

"If you came from Turtalia, then you flew over the area where they had a camp. They're trying to trace a Doradan assault team. Big things could be up. Doradans are all over the place. It looks like the buildup for an attack on the Turtalian western border."

"When did you last hear from them?" you demand.

"A week ago. Apparently they were attacked. They're still out there, I guess."

"How far from here?" you ask.

"Maybe eighty, a hundred miles. It's quicker to fly, but there is a road. We have some motorcycles. They're old, but they'll do," he responds.

If you decide to use the road to search for Matt and Mimla, turn to page 74.

If you decide to fly to the camp, turn to page 65.

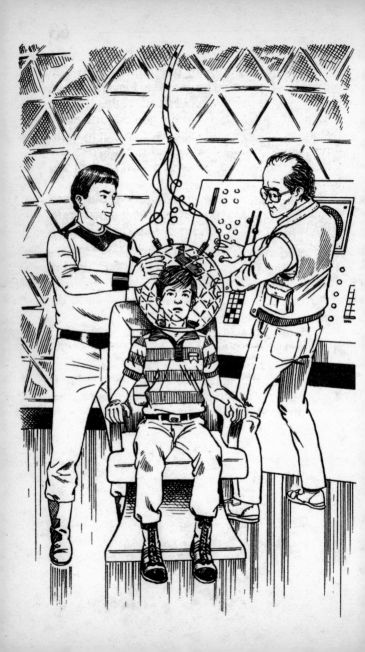

Once again, curiosity overcomes you. You agree. The humanoid form next to Haven places a clear, glasslike bell over your head. Lights snap on and off. Your head fills with the glorious and awful history of a planet and civilization far off in a different galaxy. You begin to feel the origin of the Crystal People. You become a part of their life force.

You no longer have any doubts about these creatures. Now you must try to convince others in Turtalia that the Crystal People need help. It won't be easy, but you're confident you'll succeed.

The End

"October 15, 1981," you answer. "It was a great day."

"Come with me," he replies and heads for the back part of the restaurant. Two men leave the counter and stand by the front door. You follow the waiter into a back room.

"Okay. You know the code. Now what do you want? Who are you?" Jeremy asks.

"I'm a Turtalian. I want information on Matt and Mimla, my agents. Are they safe? Where are they? When were they here last?"

"You ask a lot of questions for a stranger. If we help you, what do we get? Will Turtalia join us against the Corporation? We're desperate now."

If you decide to pledge to work against the Corporation, turn to page 61.

If you bargain with Jeremy, and avoid pledging direct Turtalian aid, turn to page 81.

"I'll fly," you say. "Get me someone who knows the area."

Jeremy nods, and returns to the restaurant counter. Moments later a woman of about fifty enters the back room. She's quite thin, but lines around her face make you think that she was fat at one time. These are hard times, and food is scarce.

The woman stares at you. Her suspicion and hostility are obvious from the look she gives you. You sense that no one here feels anyone can be trusted.

"So, you want to know where those two are, is that it?" she asks rather nastily.

"That's right. Will you show me on this map?" you reply, pushing one of your flight maps to her.

She takes it and scans it with intensity, her finger poised over the surface.

Turn to page 77.

"I'm sure the Turtalian Congress will appreciate your kind offer, Haven," you reply. "But time is of the essence, and I do have a ranger strike force that can be utilized. Perhaps a strike at their main operations base will nip this in the bud."

"As you wish, Commander, but you Earthlings do seem to make things confusing. Well, let's hope you are right. I will watch. If you need help, call." Haven dematerializes.

"I hope he's gone back inside his spacecraft," you say to Marileva. "And we'd better get moving, too. Do you have any ideas on how to proceed?"

"Why don't you and I slip into Dorado, head for the operations base, and knock it out ourselves?" she suggests. "No fuss, no mess."

You appraise the situation carefully. Two people in civilian clothes could go virtually unnoticed; a larger strike force of uniformed rangers, would not.

*If you go into Dorado with Marileva,
turn to page 72.*

*If you decide to use the whole ranger strike
force, turn to page 75.*

You're led over hilly, grassy terrain for nearly an hour. The initial excitement of the landing and of being captured wears off and fatigue sets in. After all, you flew your motorglider for over eight hours with no rest. You wish you'd finally get to wherever you're being taken.

Ten minutes later, your wish is fulfilled. You enter a camp that consists of a motley collection of tents, relics of happier times when hiking and climbing were weekend or vacation sports in California. The fabric of the tents—faded orange, yellow, tan—is worn, but they do provide shelter.

"Sit," Sellers urges you. "What do you drink? Coffee? Tea? Not that it matters. We only have herb tea, made from stuff we find along the way." He sits down next to you, and commands, "Tell your story."

Turn to page 79.

As you bounce along, you're sorry you chose the motorcycles over the plane. The highways and roads haven't been cared for in years, and they're a mass of potholes and weeds. The bikers seem oblivious to it all and merrily roar on at high speed, rocketing over the bumps and vegetation.

Turn to page 73.

"Well, a thing like this can't be decided immediately," you say. "Let me talk with my people. I can't take individual responsibility for this type of decision. Who'd believe me, anyway?"

Haven shakes his head in what looks like resignation and despair.

"So few have faith. You are not trusting your instincts. Or perhaps you are. You think this is all a Doradan hoax. I can see it in your face. Well, maybe I am wrong. Perhaps Turtalia is not for us. You are stalling, and time is precious for us now. I have wasted years on Earth already. We need help, and we need it now. You do not believe me. You do not trust me!"

Turn to page 111.

"Force begets force," you tell yourself, quoting one of the sayings of the Turtalian Congress. "I'd better wait and see what happens."

You fiddle some more with the communicator. But you haven't fooled Haven. He takes the communicator from you and puts it in his pocket.

"I will not force you to contact your base, Commander, but it is a shame that we cannot cooperate. There is much to be lost if we do not. I have a plan. Perhaps it will prove to you the seriousness of my interest in working with the Turtalian people."

You nod your head, more out of habit than in agreement with what he's just said.

"My plan is this: I will tell the Doradan commander that I am taking you back to Dorado for questioning. In reality we will go to the Turtalian capital, Denver. I cannot keep up this charade of being a Doradan agent any longer. What do you say?"

You ponder this. To bring Haven and his spacecraft to Denver using the special security codes could cause disaster to Turtalia if Haven turns out to be a fraud. He could launch a devastating strike on Turtalia.

If you decide to take Haven to Denver, turn to page 60.

If you decide to take Haven on a flight away from both Dorado and Denver, turn to page 99.

Eleven hours later you and Marileva are trapped in front of Doradan headquarters. You never had a chance. From the moment you stepped onto Doradan soil, you were doomed to failure—because of the simplest of mistakes. When you'd changed into civilian clothes, you'd forgotten to change your shoes. And Turtalian military-issue shoes leave a distinctive tread pattern that even a child can spot.

Doradans ask no questions. A blast of automatic fire ends your promising careers.

The End

"How far did you say it was?" you yell at your driver. He doesn't answer.

"How far?" you yell again.

He just grins and accelerates. The old Harley belches smoke and keeps on going.

Three hours later you cross a high pass and begin to descend into a long valley of rolling, forested hills.

You wonder why you haven't been stopped by hostile Corporation or Doradan patrols, but then, everything about this area is disorganized.

The goggles the bikers gave you are covered with dirt, and you have to keep wiping them in order to see. The exhaust fumes are making you sick to your stomach.

"How much farther?" you ask again.

The driver points ahead.

"There," he says.

Sure enough, over the next hill you come to an armed Rebel camp. The Rebels welcome the bikers, who have brought messages from people in Berkeley and a few needed supplies.

But Mimla and Matt are not there.

"Where are they?" you demand.

"They're up at the other camp with a man named Sellers," one of the men answers.

Turn to page 8.

"Motorcycles sound fine to me," you say. "Let's get going."

"Take it easy. We'll get there," says a man who's been standing in the doorway watching. "It takes time to arrange things. Be cool, man, be cool."

Several cups of herb tea later, you hear the sound of motorcycle engines. Three old Harley Davidson bikes appear. Their riders are dressed in the leather jackets of the Hell's Angels, a motorcycle club. The men are bearded and tough looking. One of the bikes has a sidecar, a little one-wheeled passenger car, attached to its side. You hope that isn't for you, but it is.

"Let's split," says one biker. He hands you a pair of goggles and a helmet.

Turn to page 68.

You are pleased to see that your ranger strike force is eager and ready to go. The effects of the tear gas have completely worn off. Equipment is checked and rechecked, and additional helicopters are called in.

It takes two hours to round up the helicopters necessary for the mission. In the meantime, you send out search teams to look for any members of the Doradan strike force who may still be in the area. None are found.

The tense, grim rangers talk little as they're airlifted deep within Doradan airspace. You're surprised that there are no Doradan air patrols. But the Doradans are busy preparing for their attack on Turtalia, and you figure that all their transports and aircraft are tied up in those preparations.

On schedule according to synchronized watches, your helicopter squadron drops out of the sky in the Doradan capital and lands near the operations building. You leap out the open helicopter door and with the others, dash for the main door. Bullets pierce the air.

Turn to page 48.

"Hands up! Don't move!" you command. They're all there—the three most important Doradans; the leaders of the Doradan army, air force, and intelligence services. "This way! Move fast!" you order. The commander of the army lunges for his weapon, but Marileva stops him with a downward smash to his forearm.

You hurry your prisoners back through the corridor, down the stairs, out into the street. Your ranger force has managed to hold off Doradan reinforcements, but their losses have been heavy. One of the helicopters has been destroyed. You, Marileva, and your prisoners, along with several rangers, board one of the remaining crafts. Moments later you're on your way out of Dorado.

A squad of Turtalian planes meets you and escorts you triumphantly home with what you hope is the biggest catch ever—the three fascist chiefs. Perhaps real peace is now possible.

The End

"There. That's where they're supposed to be. Cocky, those two, that's what they were! So sure of themselves. That's a good way to get killed. If you ask me, you're wasting your time. They've been food for the buzzards for days now, I'd say." The woman turns and leaves.

The area she pointed to on the map is right where you spotted the campfires. The problem remains—which camps are friendly?

Jeremy returns. "Got what you want, have you? Well, better leave then. You attract too much attention. Don't forget, we need help."

You nod agreement and head back to your plane. There are more people in the streets now. They move quickly and furtively.

"I'll be glad to get out of here," you say to yourself.

Turn to page 98.

So you do. Sellers nods from time to time, but he says nothing until you've finished.

"Humph! Sounds reasonable. Don't know these Matt and Mimla people, but I've heard of them. I could help if . . ."

"If what?" you ask.

"Slowly, my friend, slowly. There's a criminal gang called the Corporation in charge of what's left of San Francisco. We're Rebels—a group of freedom fighters. There are several groups like us fighting the Corporation, but we're scattered. Communication is hard. Let's make a trade, you and me, okay?"

Turn to page 82.

"The controls are useless," you shout, although there's no one to hear you.

You have no time to waste. You're only fifteen hundred feet above the ground, and the helicopter is losing altitude quickly. You wrestle with the seatbelt release. Finally, it clicks open, and you push your way through the Plexiglas door. The slipstream buffets you against the side of the helicopter. The salty taste of blood fills your mouth, the result of a nasty gash you got when you bumped your head leaving the cabin.

Whop! Your parachute snaps open and stops your tumbling fall through the murky, gas-laden cloud. You slump in the harness, legs swinging to and fro like a puppet on a string.

Moments later you're in clear air, not more than two hundred feet above the ground. Your head clears, too, and you prepare to land. There's no one around!

Where are my people? you wonder. Captain Ricardo and the rangers should be there.

Turn to page 22.

"I'm not really empowered by my government to commit us to armed involvement here. I'll see what I can do, though," you reply.

Jeremy slams his hand down on a wooden table top.

"No guts. We're fighting for our lives, and you talk like a lawyer. We don't need you or your kind. Beat it and good riddance." He turns and leaves.

What next? you think. What next? "Hey, wait a minute," you call after him. "Don't be so hasty. Let's talk. Maybe we can work something out." You hope Jeremy will be reasonable.

He turns, comes back, and looks you in the eyes.

"That's what your friends Matt and Mimla said. And what did we get? Nothing but trouble. You want to prove to us that you and Turtalia will help? Then go to the Corporation and negotiate a truce. That is, if you have the guts."

If you decide to give it a try and negotiate for a truce with the Corporation, turn to page 100.

If you decide instead to offer to lead a reconnaissance mission to survey Corporation territory, turn to page 108.

"What kind of trade?" you ask, wary of this man but half-believing his story of fighting for freedom against the criminal gang running San Francisco.

"A simple trade. You fly me to several other Rebel bases. I know where they are, or where they should be. I'll get them to help find your people, and I get to coordinate our actions against Corporation units in the area. Is it a deal?"

"If it isn't, what then?" you ask.

"We wait until you decide that you want to co-operate. We have time. That's all we have, as a matter of fact."

If you decide to take Sellers to other Rebel bases, turn to page 21.

If you decide to wait it out, turn to page 10.

"I must still be dreaming," you say as you open your eyes. Mimla is leaning over you. Matt stands beside her.

"Thank heavens you found us, Commander," Mimla says. "We've been desperate to get in touch with you. The radio equipment was smashed in our last fight with the Corporation, the San Francisco gang. How are you?"

"What? How did you get here?" you blurt out, wide awake now.

"I brought them to verify who you are," says Sellers. He's standing behind Matt. "I decided to make sure you weren't on the wrong side, so I drugged you. I knew all along where Matt and Mimla were camped. Now comes the hard part. We're surrounded by Doradan and Corporation troops. In this light it won't take them long to spot your plane and come looking for you. Then we're in the soup."

Turn to page 93.

"Now!" you say to yourself.

Grabbing the rod, you jump to your feet. With a sweeping movement, you swing the rod toward Haven.

The metal rod clangs against an impenetrable and invisible barrier and bounces back. You're knocked off your feet by the force of the rebound, landing on your back.

Turn to page 104.

86

You can't run anymore, at least not at the pace you've set. Your lungs feel as though they're about to burst. But no one seems to have noticed you. Maybe you've slipped past all the attackers.

Hunkering down on the ground beside rocks and low bushes, you catch your breath and look back at the hell you've just fled. The flashpoints of gunfire seem harmless from this distance, and the only sound is a mild popping.

"I can't rest for long," you say to yourself and start off. You walk at a fast pace following the natural contour of the hills.

Hours pass. You nibble on a mint cake and raisin bar from your kit bag for energy. Dawn is rapidly approaching, and you feel you're free of the danger zone, at least for now.

Turn to page 91.

"I'll handle Mimla and Matt," you say to the red-faced lieutenant. "Get Captain Von Moschicker over here right away. She'll take care of Haven and the files. He's a fool to think he can escape."

"Yes, Commander," the lieutenant replies. She and the other officer exit your office.

Moments later, Captain Von Moschicker snaps you a smart salute. She stands at attention waiting for your instructions. You tell her about Haven's escape and the missing files.

"Captain, take any people you need," you order, "but get Haven and those files. I have faith in you. Remember, time is of the essence. Go to it, and good luck."

"Yes, Commander. We'll do our best."

"It will have to be more than your best. You *must* recover the files," you reply.

As the captain leaves, your lieutenant enters. "Have we got a fix yet on where that message from Matt and Mimla came from?" you demand.

"Yes, Commander. One hundred miles east of San Francisco. The transmission was cut off before they completed the message."

"Okay. Get the new motorglider ready. I'm going after them," you say.

"By yourself, Commander?"

Turn to page 15.

Tension mounts as the day unfolds, and you wait uneasily for darkness to fall. The enemy patrols are in the hills all around you. The tents in the Rebel camp have been dismantled and stowed away. Everyone stays under cover. No movement is allowed.

The Rebels lie with their weapons at the ready, scanning the horizon. Occasionally there are signs of activity far off in the distance. But your area seems to be immune to discovery or attack.

Finally night comes and it's time to leave for Turtalia. With good-byes and pledges of friendship, you, Matt, and Mimla quickly head from the Rebel camp toward the field where your plane is hidden. Takeoff is chancy, but you make it and climb out of the valley. You bank and head due east. Your last look at the valley shows pinpricks of light from weapon fire. Corporation and Doradan troops are attacking the Rebel group.

Turn to page 95.

Physically, the part of Berkeley near the university seems pretty much unchanged. But many of the homes are abandoned, the people having fled to the country, afraid of the fighting between the three hostile groups.

You have a year-old map of the area provided by Turtalian intelligence. In the morning, you should be able to locate Jeremy at a restaurant called the Hungry Pelican, where he works. You decide to spend the hours until daylight in one of the abandoned houses. Once inside, you sit down and pull out your map. But before you even open it, the strain of your long flight overcomes you. Your eyes close.

Turn to page 92.

By the time daylight finally comes, you're in a pine forest on the slopes of steep hills that lead to mountains. You stop and quickly pull a map out of your kit bag. The map indicates that you're near what was once a ski resort called Squaw Valley. It might be around the next mountain.

Then you hear a noise. It's the buzzing sound of a light plane, probably an observation plane. Is it searching for you? you wonder.

If you take cover and wait until the plane leaves, turn to page 105.

If you decide to go on, trying to stay hidden in the trees, turn to page 101.

When you wake up it's morning, and the fog across the bay is beginning to lift. It's a beautiful day, but you feel lonely and sad as you walk along the empty quiet streets.

You locate the Hungry Pelican. It's open for breakfast, and twelve or fifteen people are huddled over a counter. When you enter, the babble of voices ceases immediately. Slowly faces turn to look at you. You nod a greeting, yet the silence remains unbroken.

If you decide to take a seat at the counter, turn to page 53.

If you decide to back out and wait for a better time, turn to page 96.

Matt and Mimla confirm Sellers's report.

"What are our choices?" you ask.

Sellers crouches at the tent flap and looks at the first rays of dawn over the distant mountains. "We could try to hide the plane, cover it with brush, and hope they don't spot it. Or you three could try to make it to the plane and take off. Chances are those Doradans are still asleep; they're a lazy bunch."

If you decide to try to hide the plane and wait until night before taking off, turn to page 11.

If you decide to take off immediately, turn to page 109.

You talk fast, explaining that you're a Turtalian emissary also representing the Rebels. The guard grunts and leads you into the hotel and across the lobby to the elevators. He gets on with you and punches the button for the twenty-first floor. When the doors slide open, he shoves you ahead of him into a suite of rooms. There you see a man in his thirties with a beard and long hair, wearing dark glasses, a Hawaiian shirt, an earring, and silver bracelets. He grins at you and speaks.

"Come on in. Sit down. Want something to drink? No? Well, as you wish."

Turn to page 112.

"I hope the Rebels make it," Mimla says.

You nod grimly and turn back to watch your plane's course. Silently you add your own hope that you and your agents make it as well. There's not much time left before the Doradan invasion spreads eastward.

The End

"Here I go," you say to yourself when someone coughs, and most of the faces turn toward that person. You back out the door, waving a weak good-bye to those at the counter still looking in your direction.

Whew! That smelled like trouble to me, you think.

But before you have a chance to get more than five steps away from the Hungry Pelican, a squad of thugs surrounds you.

"Looks like a spy to me, a perfect hostage," says the leader of the squad. "Take him away!"

Nylon rope is bound around your wrists, a gag is thrust in your mouth, and you're dragged away. No one comes to your aid. It's life as usual in this part of the country. True anarchy reigns. And it's said that most hostages out here don't live to tell their tale!

The End

Later that morning you're safely airborne and heading east when you pick up a radio signal. You fiddle with your radio dial until the signal clears.

"Two licorice pizzas to go. Repeat, two licorice pizzas to go."

Matt and Mimla's code call!

You respond with a six-digit identifying number, "Zero, four, two, eight, one, seven."

"We hear you. Pizza is ready for take-out," comes the response, followed by the coded coordinates of Mimla and Matt's position.

Eagerly you fly to their campsite. Now it's a matter of landing safely, taking off quickly, and avoiding Doradans on the trip home. The information Matt and Mimla have collected will no doubt help foil a Doradan attack.

The End

The security clearance codes and the coordinates with which you provide Haven lead you on a flight that ends over California. Haven is not stupid and says, "So, Commander, two can play this game."

The spacecraft leaps to hyperspace speed. You're rushed to the outer rim of the Milky Way galaxy to be interrogated by the Crystal People and used as a bargaining chip—a hostage—as they try to get what they need from Turtalia. Good luck! Turtalia has a policy never to negotiate for hostages. You've always agreed with the policy—now you aren't so sure.

The End

"Okay. I get your message," you say. "I'll see what I can do with the Corporation; you see what you can find out about Matt and Mimla. Deal?"

Jeremy grabs your hand and pumps it vigorously.

"Now, that's talking," he says.

You two spend the rest of the day planning your approach to the Corporation. Corporation headquarters is in an old hotel on Telegraph Hill.

Turn to page 106.

"I can't waste any more time," you say to yourself, and, keeping in the shadow of trees, you continue walking, hoping to escape the notice of the plane.

You wander through the Sierras for two days. At dawn of the second day you're stopped by a Rebel patrol. They bring you into headquarters, a ski-patrol shack in Squaw Valley. There you explain your mission and describe the attack on Sellers and his Rebels. Then you get the bad news.

"Your agents Matt and Mimla have been captured by Doradans," the Rebel commander tells you. "They're probably dead. You must stay with us. We're as vulnerable as Sellers and his Rebels, and we're preparing for an attack. I'm sure you can help."

The loss of your agents saddens you deeply— you must inform Operations Center as soon as possible. But for now, you know you must do as the commander says, stay with the Rebels and lend your talents to their effort to stop the Doradans.

The End

"Oh, no! Those are alien ships, not Doradan planes," you yell as you desperately attempt to dive away from the frightening fire coming from the strange craft hovering near you.

With a speed unknown to you, one of the crafts disappears.

The other two converge on you.

"Help! Help, someone, anyone! They're going to get—"

Those are the last words you ever say.

The End

Haven peers down at you.

"I do not blame you, Commander. After all, why should you trust me? Talk is cheap, as you Earth types say. I fear, though, that we have to start trusting each other sometime. Let me help you aboard the spacecraft so we can talk some more. If I give you back the files you came after, maybe you will trust me."

There's nothing to do now but go with Haven. You aren't sure whether you're a prisoner or not, but at the moment, the choices are in the hands of this being called Haven.

Talk, negotiate, plan. For now, survival is your main goal.

The End

The annoying buzzing sound comes closer and closer. The plane comes into view above the pine trees. It's an ultralight, a relic of the 1980s, when people flew the ridiculous planes for sport. Its main benefit today is that not much fuel is needed to operate it. And fuel is precious, particularly in the untamed lands of the west, which have been ravaged by fighting for years.

The ultralight zooms back and forth like a dragonfly. "What is it looking for?" you ask yourself. You realize that it's probably looking for you. But whose is it—friend or foe? Maybe Sellers got a message out to other Rebels. Maybe they're trying to help. Maybe it's even Matt and Mimla, safe and looking for you!

Just as you decide to signal the plane, it turns. The sound of the engine recedes and then is gone. You stare at the sky, and then return to the task at hand: getting out of this wilderness, finding Matt and Mimla, and getting back to Turtalia. Without your plane it's a tall order, almost impossible, but you decide not to think that way.

On you go.

The End

The next morning you leave on a mission that fills you with fear. You travel to San Francisco from Berkeley by boat. The weather is foggy and damp. The trip is long and unpleasant. You're careful to avoid Corporation patrols.

Walking through San Francisco is like moving through a nightmare. The skyscrapers are silent, many of them burned out. Windows are smashed. Rusting cars line the roads. Some of them have been burned, too. You barely escape getting caught by a patrol. But at last you make it up the long hill to the old hotel. It's a relic of the past, beautiful, elegant, and well-maintained in the midst of the destruction.

Fear almost paralyzes you as you walk up to the front door.

"What do you want?" yells a voice.

Turn to page 94.

"You're asking for too much," you say. "But I will offer to lead a mission into Corporation territory to check out the activity if you'll help me find Matt and Mimla."

Jeremy reluctantly accepts. That evening you and three of the Rebels slip across the bay by boat. Night makes San Francisco an eerie place. Here and there pinpricks of light glow from candles or lanterns. Electricity is found only in one small area at the top of a hill.

Your scouting shows you that the Corporation forces are spread out and few in number. Perhaps most of them are out in the hills with the Doradans. Or perhaps the image of the fearsome Corporation is largely the result of a big publicity campaign.

Hours later you and the Rebels return to the Hungry Pelican with your report.

"Should have known it," says Jeremy. "Phonys, they're all phonys. Well, you lived up to your bargain. We'll see what we can do about Matt and Mimla. They're out in the hills somewhere, that much we know. I'll take you there."

The End

"It's now or never," you say. "Waiting here is just asking for it."

You, Matt, and Mimla head out toward the field where the Rebels have hidden your plane. Just as you approach the field, a barrage of mortar and small-arms fire destroys the plane—and with it the hope for escape. Soon you will either be prisoners or dead. Only time will tell.

The End

Haven and the humanoid fling you from the crystal spaceship. You hit the sandy ground with a grinding thud! The ship disappears. Moments later you're surrounded by your ranger force. Your memory has begun to fade. You remember nothing about Haven and the ship. But your memory loss doesn't stop there. Soon you don't even remember who you are, where you're from, or who the people surrounding you are. Within an hour you have lost the ability to speak. All sounds become unintelligible, except for a wailing cry— and that's coming from you! You now have the mind of a three-week-old infant. Haven has taken his revenge.

The End

Behind the man are four armed guards. They watch your every move. You begin discussions with this man, whose name is Sam Osprey. He's the head of the Corporation. After much talk and bargaining, you strike a deal! All you had to do was offer him more financial help than the Doradans have offered.

"It's just cash and carry," he says, smiling.

Part of your deal is that a truce with the Rebels be declared. The other part is that Osprey help in stopping the Doradans and their plans for invading Turtalia.

You're not sure the man is trustworthy, but this is the best you can do. And it's a good start. Now you will try to find Matt and Mimla.

The End

ABOUT THE AUTHOR

R.A. MONTGOMERY is an educator and publisher. A graduate of Williams College, he also studied in graduate programs at Yale University and New York University. After serving in a variety of administrative capacities at Williston Academy and Columbia University, he co-founded Waitsfield Summer School in 1965. Following that, Montgomery helped found a research and development firm specializing in the development of educational programs. He worked for several years as a consultant to the Peace Corps in Washington, D.C., and West Africa. He is now both a writer and a publisher.

ABOUT THE ILLUSTRATOR

FRANK BOLLE studied at Pratt Institute. He has worked as an illustrator for many national magazines and now creates and draws cartoons for magazines as well. He has also worked in advertising and children's educational materials and has drawn and collaborated on several newspaper comic strips, including *Annie*. A native of Brooklyn Heights, New York, Mr. Bolle now works and lives in Westport, Connecticut.

CHOOSE YOUR OWN ADVENTURE

Prices and availability subject to change without notice.

BANTAM
SHOP-AT-HOME
C·A·T·A·L·O·G

Special Offer
Buy a Bantam Book
for only 50¢.

Now you can order the exciting books you've been
wanting to read straight from Bantam's latest
listing of hundreds of titles. *And* this special offer
gives you the opportunity to purchase a Bantam
book for only 50¢. Here's how:

By ordering any five books at the regular price
per order, you can also choose any other single
book listed (up to $4.95 value) for only 50¢. Some
restrictions do apply, so for further details send
for Bantam's listing of titles today.

Just send us your name and address and we'll send
you Bantam Book's SHOP AT HOME CATALOG!